5-
MINUTE
Biscuit
STORIES

written by Alyssa Satin Capucilli
illustrated by Pat Schories

HARPER FESTIVAL
An Imprint of HarperCollinsPublishers

For Pete and Kate

and the start of many stories!

—A.S.C.

5-Minute Biscuit Stories
Text copyright © 2017 by Alyssa Satin Capucilli
Illustrations copyright © 2017 by Pat Schories

ISBN 978-0-06-256725-3

Typography by Lori S. Malkin
17 18 19 20 21   SCP   10 9 8 7 6 5 4 3 2
❖
First edition

Contents

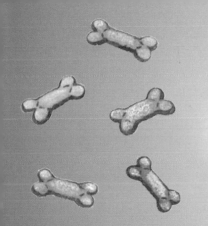

Meet Biscuit!

Today was a special day. Today the little girl could bring her new puppy home. When Aunt Clara and Uncle Henry's dog had a litter of pups, Aunt Clara promised the little girl she could choose one for her own. She picked a small yellow puppy! Now, after waiting eight long weeks for it to be old enough, the day had come at last! The little girl could hardly wait to pick a name for her new pup!

5

The little girl carefully took her puppy out of the box she carried him in. Aunt Clara had tucked his favorite blanket right inside. The blanket had the scent of the puppy's brothers and sisters. A familiar scent would help him get used to his new home.

"Here we are, puppy," said the little girl. "Welcome to your new home!"

Woof, woof!

"Here is your shiny red collar," said the little girl. "It fits perfectly!"

Woof, woof!

"Wait, little puppy.
Where are you going?"
Woof!

It took only a moment for the little puppy to get busy sniffing his new surroundings. Puppies use their noses to learn about everything around them. He quickly found his kibble and water bowl.

"What a funny puppy you are," said the little girl as he rolled around on the rug. The new pup pulled and tugged at her shoelaces. He licked her cheek. But when he started to nip at her shirt, she said, "No nipping."

Aunt Clara had said it might take time to teach the puppy new tricks like sitting and fetching. Still, it was important to teach him right from wrong.

"This way, sweet puppy," said the little girl. "The first thing we must do is find a name for you."

Woof, woof!

It was fun having the puppy follow behind her. He seemed to understand everything she said to him!

"Let's see. You are small and yellow. . . ."

Woof, woof!

"Wait a minute," said the little girl. "Where are you going, silly puppy? Come back here!"

Woof!

"You found your cozy bed and your bone. You even found a box of dog biscuits!"

Woof, woof!

"I can see you are very curious. But no biscuits yet," she said. "Before you do any more exploring, I think we should try to find a name for you."

The little girl got her chalkboard.
Maybe if she wrote it down, they would
find just the right name for the pup.

"Let's see. You are small and
yellow. . . . How about . . . Tiny? Here,
Tiny," she called.

The puppy sat down and scratched
his ear!

"No. Tiny is not quite right."

Next the little girl wrote down
"Sunny."

"Fetch, Sunny." She rolled a small
ball to her pup. "No. That's not the
right name, either."

Woof, woof!

"Wait, little puppy! Where are you
going now?" she asked.

Woof, woof!

"You found your doll and new toys. And you found your box of dog biscuits again! But no tugging now. That box of biscuits is too big for you."

Woof, woof!

The little girl gently carried the new puppy over to her chalkboard. She brought his favorite blanket and some of his toys. His fur felt so soft and warm against her cheek!

"See?" said the little girl. "You have everything a puppy could need. Everything except a name, that is!"

Woof, woof!

"Now, let's try again. What is your name going to be?"

First she wrote down "F-I-D-O."

"Fido might be a good name for you."

Next she wrote down "R-E-X."

"Or maybe Rex? Rex is a great name for a puppy."

Woof!

The puppy was too busy to sit still for long.

He wanted to discover more about his new home.

"Uh-oh! You're off exploring again!" she said.

"Silly puppy! How did you get that box of biscuits?"

Woof, woof!

"Oh no!" called the little girl. "Come back here with those biscuits!"

Woof, woof, woof, woof!

As the puppy ran with the box, biscuits tumbled out here and there.

"You may be a small yellow puppy, but I'm afraid you are a bit mischievous, too! Just look. There are dog biscuits everywhere!"

Woof, woof!

"Wait a minute," said the little girl. "Biscuits? Biscuits everywhere? Biscuit! That's it! Biscuit is the perfect name for you! You are small and yellow and the very sweetest puppy I have ever met.

"Hello, Biscuit! You found a name all by yourself!"
Woof, woof!

After all that running, exploring, and chasing, Biscuit curled up in his bed with his blanket.

"I will always take very good care of you, sleepy puppy," whispered the little girl. She could hardly wait to take Biscuit to the pond and the park and the playground.

Maybe one day she would even take Biscuit to school! But for now, she gave Biscuit a big hug and a big kiss, too. He was still a very young puppy, and puppies need a lot of rest.

Now that he was getting used to his new home, there was just one thing left to do. It was time to call Aunt Clara and Uncle Henry. Wait until they heard her new puppy's name . . . Biscuit!

Biscuit Meets the Class Pet

Biscuit stood in his cozy bed and sniffed the air. There was a new scent in the house. What could it be? Biscuit hurried inside just as the little girl called to him.

There *was* something new in the house. Something he had never seen before!

"Here, Biscuit," said the little girl. "Come and meet Nibbles!"

Woof, woof!

Biscuit padded over to where the little girl was sitting. She was holding a small gray-and-white bunny in her arms. It was very fuzzy!

"This is Nibbles," said the little girl. "He is our class pet. We must take very good care of him while he is visiting this weekend. My teacher gave me plenty of food for Nibbles. He needs lots of fresh water every day, too."

Woof, woof!

Biscuit sniffed at Nibbles's hutch. Then he sniffed at the little bunny. Biscuit always liked to make a new friend. Now Nibbles sniffed back at Biscuit. The little bunny wiggled his small pink nose. He wiggled his ears, too. Then with one big hop, Nibbles leaped from the little girl's arms.

"Nibbles is a very curious bunny," said the little girl. "I think he is ready to explore his new surroundings!"

Hop, hop!

Nibbles may have been a curious bunny, but Biscuit was a very curious puppy! He wanted to get to know Nibbles. He hoped the little bunny would want to play.

"Look, Biscuit!" called the little girl. "Nibbles found your bone."

Woof, woof!

Biscuit hurried over to the soft, white ball of fur. He was happy to share his bone with Nibbles.

But Nibbles wasn't interested in Biscuit's bone for long.
In no time at all, Nibbles twitched his soft ears
and hopped over to Biscuit's striped ball.
Then he hopped right
over to Biscuit's bed.
Hop, hop!
Woof, woof!

Now Biscuit climbed into his cozy bed. He gathered his favorite blanket in his mouth. Maybe Nibbles would like to play tug! That was Biscuit's favorite game.

"Silly puppy! I'm afraid bunnies don't play tug," the little girl said, laughing.

She turned to Biscuit and said, "Stay here, Biscuit. At school I learned that Nibbles enjoys a carrot or some lettuce every now and then. I'm going to get a snack for Nibbles. You can keep an eye on him."

Woof, woof!

But just as the little girl left the room, Nibbles
wiggled his nose and set out to explore some more.

Hop, hop!

Woof!

Nibbles moved so quickly. No matter how he
tried, it was difficult for Biscuit to keep up with
the little bunny. Biscuit followed closely behind
until Nibbles hopped beneath the table. But in only
moments, Nibbles scurried out and set off again.
Woof, woof!

With one big hop, Nibbles disappeared from sight. Which way did he go? Biscuit looked all around the room until at last he found a clue.

There was a small fluffy tail poking out from under the big green chair. Biscuit hurried over at once, but already, Nibbles was nowhere to be found!
Woof, woof!

Biscuit was certain he had seen Nibbles there just a moment ago. The puppy was busy sniffing under the chair when the little girl returned with a crunchy carrot for Nibbles.

"Oh no, Biscuit!" said the little girl. "Where is Nibbles? We have to find him. We are supposed to take very good care of him while he is visiting."

Woof, woof!

Biscuit wanted to take good care of the fuzzy bunny, too. The search was on!

First the little girl and Biscuit checked under the table again, but Nibbles was not there. They looked on top of the big green chair and searched every corner of the room.

"Maybe Nibbles is hiding behind the pillow," said the little girl. But no, Nibbles was not there, either.

"Oh, Biscuit," said the little girl with a sigh. "I didn't know babysitting a bunny could be so difficult."

Woof!

Biscuit lifted his nose into the air. He sniffed around and around. He sniffed at the ground, too. Then Biscuit began to run.

Woof, woof!

"Wait for me, Biscuit!" called the little girl as Biscuit ran to his cozy bed.

"Funny puppy," said the little girl. "It's not time to nap now. It's time to find Nibbles."

But Biscuit wasn't ready for a nap at all. Without making a sound, he climbed into his bed and lay his head on his paws. There was the small gray-and-white ball of fur they had been searching for. Gently, Biscuit touched his nose to Nibbles's nose. Nibbles wiggled his nose. He twitched his ears, too.

"You may be the best bunny-sitter in the world, Biscuit!" said the little girl. "Nibbles may have found your bone and your ball and your bed, but you found Nibbles!"

Woof, woof!

Biscuit gathered his favorite blanket in his mouth. Bunnies might not like to play tug, but he was happy to share all that he had with his new friend, Nibbles.

"I bet Nibbles will miss you when I bring him back to our classroom, Biscuit," said the little girl, laughing. "But who knows? Maybe one day you can come for a visit, too!"

Woof, woof!

Biscuit's First Trip

It was time to take a family trip. There was sure to be plenty of wintertime fun. The little girl looked forward to sledding and skating with her cousins. Most of all, she was excited that Biscuit was coming along, too. Where was that funny puppy anyway?

"Biscuit, where are you?" called the little girl.

Woof, woof!

"Come along, sweet puppy! Today is a very special day," said the little girl. "We're going on a trip with our family."

Woof, woof!

"Let's get ready, Biscuit," said the little girl. She set her red suitcase out on the bed. "The first thing we must do is pack our bag. Pajamas—check. Sweaters—check. Toothbrush, hairbrush, books, and music—check. I'll take along my favorite doll, too. And you have your blanket and your bone."

Woof, woof!

This was the first time Biscuit had gone on a family vacation. The little girl knew her puppy would have a wonderful time. Still, she wanted to make sure she had everything her puppy would need.

When the last suitcase had been packed, the family climbed into the car and set out on their trip. The little girl opened her map to see just which direction they were headed.

"It's fun to take a trip, Biscuit," said the little girl. "The car ride may be long, but we can share stories and sing songs. Even the baby can sing along!"

Biscuit was already very busy looking out of the car window.

Woof, woof!

"Funny puppy!" said the little girl. "You found some horses and cows. There will be a lot more to see along the way."

Woof!

When they had driven for some time, they stopped at a scenic lookout point. It was a great place to take photographs of the beautiful scenery.

"Look, Biscuit," said the little girl. "There are tall mountains, rolling hills, and lots of trees."

But Biscuit had found something, too.
Woof!
"Oh, Biscuit. That's a chipmunk," she said.
After the family had stretched their legs, they climbed back into the car.

Soon they arrived at the snow-covered inn
where the rest of their family was waiting.
The little girl was glad she had remembered
to pack her hat and mittens!

"Hooray! We're here at last," she said. "This
way, Biscuit. There's Grandma and Grandpa. Aunt
Clara, Uncle Henry, and our cousins are here, too.
We're going to have a lot of fun on this trip."
Woof, woof!
Biscuit couldn't agree more. He wagged his tail
and ran ahead to give hugs and kisses to everyone!

Soon it was time for the
fun-filled vacation to begin. The little girl and her
cousins carried their sleds to the top of a small hill. She
gathered Biscuit snugly in her lap.

"Hold on, Biscuit. Off we go!" she cried. Down, down,
down the hill went the sled.

Woof!

Biscuit could feel the brisk wind blowing against his
ears. Sledding was fun, especially when they landed in
the crunchy snow!

But there was more fun to come.

Later in the day, they built a family of snowmen and made snow angels. There was even time to visit the ice-skating pond. The only problem was, the ice was very slippery for a small puppy. Biscuit tried to walk on the ice, but he kept falling down.

"Be careful, Biscuit," called the little girl. "The ice may be too slippery for you."

Woof, woof!

The next morning, everyone set out for a long walk in the woods. Taking a walk was one of Biscuit's favorite things to do.

"This way, Biscuit," said the little girl. "I have my binoculars. We'll be able to take a very close look at everything."

It was interesting to look at the many footprints in the snow made by rabbits, deer, and squirrels that made their home in the woods. They discovered pine trees and birch

trees. They even saw a red cardinal perched on a tree
branch. Its feathers looked especially bright against the
dazzling white snow.

"And you found a pinecone, Biscuit!" said the little girl.
Woof, woof!

When the sun began to set, everyone returned to the
inn. A golden fire crackled in the fireplace, warming their
fingers and toes. It felt good on Biscuit's paws, too.

Sitting by the fire, the family enjoyed
hot apple cider, doughnuts—and a bone
especially for Biscuit!

After a good night's sleep, the next morning brought a special family treat.

Jingle-jingle! Jingle-jingle!

"Oh, Biscuit," said the little girl. "We're going on a horse-drawn sleigh ride!"

"Climb aboard, everyone, and bundle up!" called the little girl's mom.

"Cuddle up, sweet puppy," said the little girl. "It's beginning to snow."

Jingle-jingle! Jingle-jingle!

Woof, woof, woof, woof!

The jingle of the horse's bells was the perfect sound as they snuggled under blankets and rode across the snow-covered hills.

Back at the inn, everyone gathered together for a family picture. It would be a wonderful memory of the trip they had taken together.

"There's nothing quite like spending time with our family, is there, Biscuit?" said the little girl. She linked her arm with Grandma's and kept her sweet puppy by her side.

"Smile, everyone. This is one trip we'll always want to remember," she said. "And one picture that's going right into my scrapbook!"

Woof, woof!

Biscuit in the Garden

The little girl gathered her bucket and her gardening tools. It was sunny and warm outside; it was a perfect day to work in the garden. She always enjoyed digging and planting with her puppy by her side. Even more fun was discovering the many small creatures that made the garden their home.

"Come along, Biscuit. It's time to visit the garden. Are you ready to help with some digging and planting?" she asked.

Woof, woof!

Biscuit wagged his tail with excitement. He was already busy sniffing around the toolshed.

"The garden is filled with so many things, Biscuit," said the little girl. "Just look at all the flowers and plants."

Woof, woof!

Usually Biscuit loved to explore the flowers and plants, especially when there wasn't a bee buzzing nearby!

But right now, there was something beautiful and yellow with soft fluttering wings tickling his nose.

Woof, woof!

"You found a butterfly, Biscuit," said the little girl.

But that wasn't all. No sooner had the butterfly set off into the sky than Biscuit found another garden critter.

Biscuit crouched low to the ground to watch a long wiggly worm slowly inching by.

Woof!

The worm quickly burrowed into the soil and out of sight!

"This way now, Biscuit," said the little girl. She gathered her bucket and spade. "I have some digging to do over here. Some of these flowers are even bigger than you are, sweet puppy!"

Digging was something Biscuit liked to do, too. He got busy at once, tossing the dirt far and wide!

"Silly puppy!" said the little girl. "Don't dig up the flowers now . . . please!"

Woof, woof!

Biscuit was ready to explore some more when he heard a bird calling overhead.

Tweet! Tweet!

There was a bright-blue bird circling around the garden. Every so often, the bird swooped down close to Biscuit, then it flew up and pecked at the bird feeder.

Woof!

"Look, Biscuit," said the little girl.
"The bird is right by the bird feeder.
Maybe the little bird is hungry."
Woof, woof!
"Let's feed the bird, Biscuit. I
know we have plenty of birdseed in
the shed," said the little girl. "Wait
here, Biscuit."

As Biscuit waited for the little girl to return, he saw two more birds hovering by the bird feeder. The little girl soon appeared, pulling a large sack behind her.

Woof, woof!

"Wait, Biscuit. What do you see now?" she asked.

Woof!

"Oh, Biscuit," she said. "There are two more little birds! I guess everyone in the garden is hungry this morning. It's a good thing we have plenty of birdseed."

Biscuit watched as the little girl scooped out the birdseed and stretched on her tiptoes to fill the bird feeder.

"Here, little birds," she called. "Here is some crunchy birdseed. Come and get it!"

Tweet! Tweet!

Woof, woof!
Now more birds flew into the garden and surrounded the bird feeder. Biscuit was curious. He stood on his hind legs and sniffed at the large sack.
Woof, woof!

"Come along now, Biscuit," said the little girl. "The birds are busy eating, and there is more work to be done in the garden. There's lots more to see, too."

But Biscuit was still busy exploring something right where he was. If only he could see inside that large sack of birdseed.

Biscuit stretched as high as he could on his hind legs. He leaned forward and let the scent of the birdseed fill his nose. He tried to inch just a bit closer but with just one step . . .

CRASH! The whole bag of birdseed toppled over, spilling onto the ground!

"Oh no, Biscuit!" said the little girl. "Not the birdseed!"

Tweet! Tweet! Tweet! Tweet!

Woof, woof! Woof, woof!

In only a moment, birds of every size flocked to the garden, diving and pecking at the large pile of birdseed! Biscuit ran playfully alongside the colorful birds.

"Oh, Biscuit," said the little girl. "There is birdseed on your nose and your paws. There is birdseed just about everywhere!"

Woof, woof!

But the little girl couldn't be angry at her mischievous puppy for long. The birdseed had brought birds of all kinds from far and wide. There were blue jays and cardinals; there were sparrows, robins, and finches. All of them had come to their garden for a most delicious meal.

"Just look at all the birds now, Biscuit!" said the little girl.
"I'm not even sure I can count them all." She giggled.

Biscuit soon discovered that while birdseed may have been tasty to the birds, it was not nearly as delicious a treat as his bone.

Still, it was fun to watch the birds flying all about. Of course, it was fun to chase after them, too.

Tweet! Tweet! Tweet! Tweet!

Woof, woof! Woof, woof!

"The garden is filled with flowers and plants and so many amazing living things, Biscuit," said the little girl. "But you filled the garden with lots of birds, too!"

Biscuit scampered over to the little girl. He loved helping her in the garden. He loved discovering all sorts of critters and creatures. He loved playing with the colorful birds. Most of all, Biscuit loved giving the little girl a great big kiss—filled with birdseed!

Woof, woof!

Biscuit Takes a Walk

One beautiful fall morning, the little girl decided to take a walk to Grandpa's house. It was always fun to walk there, with plenty to see, hear, and smell along the way.

Still, the little girl knew her walk would be even more fun if her small yellow puppy, Biscuit, came along, too! He was always ready for a new adventure. The little girl quickly tied her sneakers and went to find Biscuit's leash.

"It's a nice, sunny day, Biscuit," said the little girl.
"Would you like to take a walk to Grandpa's house?"

Woof, woof!

Biscuit pulled at his leash. Taking a walk was one of his favorite things to do!

"Silly puppy! No tugging on the leash now," the little girl said, laughing. She hugged her favorite puppy close to her.

"Are you ready, Biscuit?" she asked. "Let's go!"

Woof, woof!

Biscuit walked right by the little girl's side.
He could feel the soft breeze tickling his tail! But
their walk had only just begun when Biscuit saw
some fresh brown dirt. To Biscuit, fresh brown
dirt meant it was time for digging. Dirt
was soon flying everywhere!

Woof, woof!

"Oh no, Biscuit. No digging now," said the little girl. "We are taking a walk to Grandpa's house."

Woof, woof!

Biscuit wagged his tail and got back on the path. But they hadn't gone too far when Biscuit saw a bed of flowers. Its scent wafted right over to Biscuit's keen nose. Was there anything more fun for a puppy than rolling in a sweet-smelling bed of flowers? Biscuit couldn't resist. Into the flower bed he went!

Woof, woof!

"Funny puppy," said the little girl. "It's not time to roll.
It's time to take a walk to Grandpa's house."

Woof, woof!

Biscuit loved to take a walk. He loved to visit Grandpa.
He was back at the little girl's side at once. Until . . .

Chee-chee! Chee-chee!

What was that sound? Being a very curious puppy, Biscuit had to find out!

Woof!

"Those are squirrels, Biscuit," said the little girl.

Chee-chee! Chee-chee!

The squirrels were playing in the tree. Could he play, too?

Woof, woof!

But, no. The squirrels were not ready to play with a puppy. They quickly climbed the branches and scurried out of sight.

"Come along now, Biscuit. If we keep stopping, we'll never get to Grandpa's house," said the little girl.

Woof, woof!

The little girl and Biscuit walked and walked. They
felt the warm sun on their faces. They saw thick, fluffy
clouds floating by.

"That's the way, Biscuit," said the little girl. "I know
Grandpa will be very excited to see us."

But then came another interesting sound.

Tweet!

Biscuit's ears perked up. What could that be?

Tweet! Tweet!

There, just ahead, was a small flock of birds. Biscuit
knew that chasing birds was always sure to be fun.

Woof, woof!

"Wait, Biscuit. Come back," called the little girl.

Biscuit ran toward the birds. But he did not stop there.
He tugged and pulled on his leash until he broke free!

"Biscuit, where are you going?" she called.

Woof, woof, woof, woof!

Biscuit ran and ran until he came to a large store. Then he stopped. He stood on his hind legs and peered into the store window.

Woof, woof!

"Oh, Biscuit," said the little girl. "This is not Grandpa's house. This is the grocery store. Come on, Biscuit. Grandpa's house is this way."

The little girl gently tugged on Biscuit's leash. But no matter how she tried, Biscuit wouldn't budge! Now with one big pull, Biscuit hurried inside the grocery store.

Biscuit ran past the cheeses and meats at the deli counter. He ran past the bread, the muffins, and the cupcakes. Biscuit even ran past the bones, the balls, and the chew toys.

Woof, woof, woof, woof!

Biscuit was running so fast!

"Biscuit!" she called. "We are supposed to take a walk to Grandpa's house. We aren't supposed to go grocery shopping!"

Woof!

And when the little girl finally saw Biscuit in the distance, she knew at once just what her funny puppy was after. It wasn't a bone. It wasn't a ball or a chew toy, either. It was Grandpa!

The little girl hugged Biscuit tightly. She gave Grandpa a big hug, too.

"What a wonderful surprise this is," said Grandpa, lifting Biscuit into his shopping cart.

"We were taking a walk to see you, Grandpa," said the little girl. "But Biscuit found you even before we got to your house."

"Well now," said Grandpa. "It is a beautiful sunny day, and a perfect day for a walk, too. I guess this will be a walk for all of us."

The little girl held Grandpa's hand tightly as they walked to his house.

"Grandma thought I was just going shopping for groceries," said Grandpa. "But won't she be happy when she sees the surprise I'm bringing home!"

Woof, woof!

"Lead the way, Biscuit," said Grandpa.

"A walk to your house is a lot of fun, Grandpa," said the little girl. "But a walk with you is the very best walk of all. Right, Biscuit?"

Woof, woof!

Biscuit's Big Friend

Today the little girl was having a playdate with one of her best friends. Not only would the two girls spend the day together, but their dogs, Biscuit and Sam, could play together, too.

The little girl found Biscuit's leash and called to her favorite puppy, "Here, Biscuit. It's time to go to Sam's house."

Woof, woof!

Biscuit was at her side in a moment. Even though Sam was a very big dog and Biscuit was a small puppy, the two dogs were very good friends. When they arrived at Sam's, the big dog curled up on the ground and touched his nose to Biscuit's nose. It was Biscuit's favorite way of being greeted by his big, gentle friend. But they didn't sit quietly for long!

Ruff!

Biscuit stood on his hind legs. He did his best to climb up onto his big friend Sam! Biscuit was just about to hop onto Sam's back when . . .

Sam wagged his tail and began to run. Sam ran fast!
In a moment, he was clear across the yard.

Woof, woof!

Biscuit wanted to run fast, too! He followed behind
Sam as best he could, but his legs were just too small
to keep up.

Ruff!

Now Sam found a big stick. He lifted it in his mouth
and carried it over to Biscuit.

Woof, woof!

Biscuit wanted to carry a big stick, too. He tried to

lift the stick with all his might, but there were just
some things a small puppy could not do.

"Funny puppy!" said the little girl. "That stick
is just too big and heavy for you to lift all by
yourself." She gave Biscuit a smaller stick
to hold instead.

Next it was time to play tug. Sam held one end of the rope in his mouth while Biscuit held the other. Sam knew to be gentle with his friend. But even the smallest tug from Sam made it hard for Biscuit to hold on. Biscuit tried to tug back, but Sam won the game every time.

Ruff, ruff!
Woof, woof!
"Here, Biscuit," said the little girl, laughing, as the dogs tugged and tugged. "Maybe I can help you with a tug or two!"
Woof!

After all of that running
and tugging, the girls knew that
their dogs should have a cool drink.
"Here, Biscuit! Here, Sam! Come and get it!" the girls called.

Biscuit padded over to his water bowl. It was just the right size for a small puppy. But when he saw Sam lapping up water from a much bigger bowl, Biscuit hurried to Sam's side. He wanted to do everything his big friend could do. Biscuit climbed up to reach Sam's bowl, but just as he was about to take his first sip of water . . . SPLASH! He tumbled right inside the big bowl!

"Silly puppy!" said the little girl. "Sam's bowl is too big for you!"

Woof, woof!
Ruff! Ruff!

After a great big shake, it was time to think of what to do next on this puppy playdate!

"I know. Let's play fetch," said the little girl. "We can throw the ball, and you two can bring it back. Ready?"

The little girl found a small ball and threw it as far as she could.

"Fetch it, Sam! Fetch the ball, Biscuit!" the girls called.

Ruff!

Woof!

Sam ran as fast as he could. Biscuit ran as fast as he could, too.

The two dogs chased after the ball as it soared through the air. Up, up, up the ball went until it landed . . . right over the neighbor's fence!

"Uh-oh!" said the little
girl. "There goes the ball."

"Now what will we do?"
asked her friend.

Ruff!

Sam ran toward the fence. He looked as if he might jump!

"Wait, Sam!" the girls called. "That fence is too big, even
for you!"

Sam was a very big dog, but the fence was still too high to
jump over. He stood on his hind legs and barked at the ball!

Ruff, Ruff! Ruff, Ruff!

But now the girls heard a loud *Woof!*

It was Biscuit! Biscuit was running toward the fence at full
speed! Would he try to jump over the fence, too?

"Biscuit, where are you going?" called the little girl. "That fence is much too big for you."

Woof, woof!

Biscuit came to a halt just as he reached the fence. He sniffed at the ground. And although Biscuit was a small puppy, he had an idea—a big idea that would surprise everyone! Biscuit may not have been big enough to jump over the fence, but he was small enough to crawl under the fence.

Woof, woof!

"Oh, Biscuit! You did it!" said the little girl.

"That's the way to fetch the ball. Only a small puppy like you could do that!" she added, giving him a big hug.

Ruff!

Sam got a big hug, too, then he lay in the cool grass with Biscuit. Biscuit was ready to play another game. Holding his striped ball in his mouth, he hoped Sam was ready to play again soon.

Big or small, Biscuit and Sam were very good friends. And that was the most important thing of all.

Woof, woof!

Ruff!

Biscuit and the Baby

Early one morning, Biscuit awoke and gave himself a big stretch. He looked over to where the little girl slept. Most mornings she woke her puppy with a big hug, but today, her bed was empty. Where could the little girl be?
Biscuit stretched once more, then he picked up his ball and set out to find her. The little girl was always ready to play.

When he found her at last, Biscuit dropped his ball at her feet and wagged his tail.

Woof, woof!

But instead of being ready to play, the little girl put her finger to her mouth and whispered, "Shhh. Be very quiet, Biscuit. We have a brand-new baby in the house. Babies need a lot of sleep. We must be careful not to wake the baby," said the little girl. "Come on, Biscuit, you can follow me."

Biscuit followed the little girl into the
bedroom. He watched as she climbed onto the bed and
peeked at the small bundle in her mother's arms.

"Can I hold the baby?" asked the little girl.

Her mother smiled. She put a large pillow on the little
girl's lap. Then she carefully passed the small bundle into
the little girl's arms. Biscuit was curious. Who was this
new baby? What was a baby anyway?

Biscuit liked the soft song the little girl's mother was
singing. He liked the sweet scent that filled the air, too.

Woof, woof!

Biscuit wanted to meet the baby! But the little girl
held her finger to her mouth once again. She stroked
Biscuit's soft yellow fur.

"Shhh! Quiet, Biscuit," she whispered. "The baby
is sleeping. It's not time to meet the baby yet."

Biscuit looked around. The room was filled with so many new and interesting things. Being a very curious puppy, Biscuit set out to explore at once.

Woof!

First Biscuit found a bright-green ball on the floor. If he couldn't meet the baby, maybe the little girl would play ball. He carried the ball over and dropped it into the little girl's lap.

"Oh no, Biscuit," said the little girl. "That's not your ball. That's the baby's rattle."

Biscuit carried the rattle toward the baby's bassinet. But on the way, he saw something else that looked like fun. It was a stuffed bunny. Biscuit gathered the little toy in his mouth. He carried it over to where the baby was still fast asleep.

"Oh, Biscuit," said the little girl. "Now you found the baby's bunny."

Woof, woof!

"Shhh! You must remember to be very quiet, Biscuit," said the little girl. "The baby is still sleeping. It's not time to meet the baby yet."

Biscuit rolled onto his back. He looked around. If it wasn't time to play with the little girl, and it wasn't time to meet the baby, there must be something else he could do. Just then, Biscuit saw a cozy yellow blanket on the bed. With one jump, he pulled the blanket right off the bed and began to run!

Woof, woof!

"Silly puppy!" said the little girl. "That's not your blanket. That blanket is for the baby."

Just then, something else caught his eye. With a quick pounce, Biscuit found two tiny white booties. But when he lifted them into his mouth, the little girl was right there to take them away.

"Oh no, Biscuit," she said. "Those booties are for the baby. Booties keep the baby's tiny feet nice and warm."

Woof, woof!

"Funny puppy! You want to meet the baby. But babies need a lot of sleep. I'm afraid it's not time to meet the baby yet. I'll give you a little peek, but be very quiet, Biscuit," said the little girl. She lifted Biscuit into her arms and hugged him close to her.

"See, sweet puppy?" she said. "The baby is still fast asleep."

Biscuit looked at the tiny baby. And although he didn't mean to do it, Biscuit gave one large and loud *Woof!*

And just then, there was a sound Biscuit had never heard before!

Waa! Waa! Waa! Waa!

"Oh no, Biscuit," said the little girl. "Now we've woken up the baby!"

Waa! Waa! The baby cried and cried.

Woof! Woof! Woof! Woof!

Biscuit was afraid of
such a loud sound. He quickly
wriggled out of the little girl's
arms and scrambled underneath
the bed.

"Biscuit, where are you?" called the little girl.

Now Biscuit peeked out from under the bed. There
was the little girl, smiling at him.

"Oh, Biscuit," she said. "I bet that sound frightened you.
But you don't have to hide under the bed. It's only the baby!
Come back, Biscuit."

Woof, woof!

Biscuit watched as the little girl's mom lifted the baby into her arms. She rocked the baby. She gave the baby lots of hugs and kisses. She sang a soft song, too, until the baby had quieted down. Now the little girl lifted Biscuit into her arms. She rocked him. She sang a soft song to him. Of course, Biscuit got lots of hugs and kisses, too.

"Here, sweet puppy," said the little girl. She carried Biscuit over to where her mom was gently rocking the baby.

"Now it's time to meet the baby, Biscuit," she said. "And best of all, it's time for the baby to meet a new friend! It's time for the baby to meet you, sweet puppy."

Biscuit looked at the tiny baby. He sniffed at the baby's fingers and toes.

"That's the way, Biscuit. I'm sure that you and the baby are going to be very good friends," said the little girl.

Woof, woof!

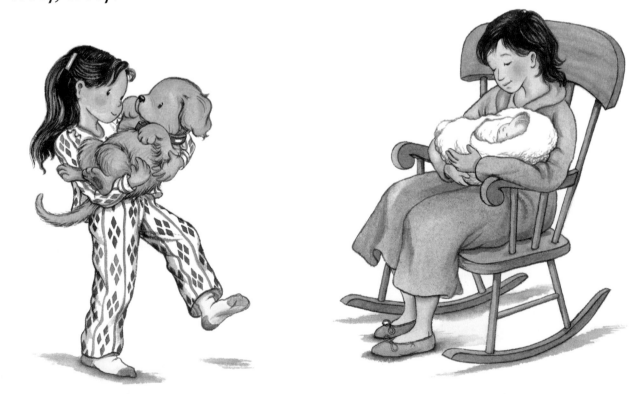

Biscuit's Day at the Farm

It was always fun to visit Aunt Clara and Uncle Henry's farm. There were animals of every kind. The little girl loved riding the horses and watching the cows as they grazed in the grass. The spring was the most special time at the farm, and the best time to visit. There were so many baby animals to see. Best of all, Aunt Clara always welcomed the little girl's help. Today Uncle Henry gave her a bucket filled with grain. It was feeding time on the farm, and there were plenty of animals to be fed. She could hardly wait to begin!

"Come along, Biscuit," called the little girl. "We're going to help on the farm today."

Woof, woof!

Biscuit was already busy sniffing at the
chicken coop. The hens were clucking happily while
their chicks made soft peeping sounds.

The little girl sprinkled the golden grain and was quickly
surrounded by the hens. Next it was time to feed the pigs.

With a wag of his tail, Biscuit scurried outside to where the pig
was resting. Some of her piglets were snuggled by her side.
Others were busy exploring the rest of the pen.

"Funny puppy," said the little girl, "you found the pig
and the piglets, too."

Woof!

Biscuit stood on his hind legs. He found himself face-to-face with a tiny piglet. Biscuit nearly squeezed inside the pigpen. He always liked to make a new friend.

"Uncle Henry is giving the piglets fresh water, Biscuit," said the little girl. "But come along. We have lots more to do, too. Let's feed the goats."

Woof, woof!

The little girl and Biscuit entered the large stall where the goats were busy playing.

Maa-maa! Maa-maa! the goats called to each other!

But just as the little girl and Biscuit began to feed the goats, they heard an unlikely sound—a sound that did not belong to a goat at all!

Oink!

"Oh, Biscuit," said the little girl, "I'm afraid the tiny piglet is out of the pen."

Woof!

Biscuit wagged his tail. The little piglet was just the right size to be a perfect playmate. But before he could run or tug or play, the little girl scooped the piglet up into her arms.

"This way, Biscuit," she said. "We must put the piglet back in the pen." Back to its pen the piglet went.

"Now stay put, sweet piglet," said the little girl. "It's time for us to feed the sheep."

It was fun to feed the sheep. Their coats were soft and woolly. The little girl liked their calls of *baa, baa*. But just as they set out clean hay for the sheep, there came another *Oink!*

"Oh no, Biscuit," moaned the little girl. "It's the piglet! How did that piglet find us again?"

Woof!

Now Biscuit really wanted to play with the piglet.

"I'm sorry, sweet puppy," said the little girl. "We must put the piglet back one more time."

Gently, the little girl held the piglet in her arms. Together they brought the piglet back to the pen where the rest of the litter was busy at play.

"In you go," said the little girl. "We will come back and visit you when we're finished feeding the rest of the animals."

Woof, woof!

Now that the piglet was safely back in its pen, there was more work to be done. The little girl brought Biscuit over to where the geese were waiting to be fed.

"Here are the geese, Biscuit," she said.

Woof, woof!

Honk! Honk! Honk! Honk!

Biscuit wanted to meet the geese, but their loud call frightened him a bit. Biscuit hid behind the little girl's legs. And when the little girl turned to comfort Biscuit, she saw another familiar face!

Oink!

The piglet had wandered out of its pen and found them again!

To make matters worse, the little girl accidentally opened the goose pen. The geese began to run!

Honk! Honk!

Now Biscuit began to run, too!

"Wait, Biscuit," called the little girl. "The geese are just saying hello."

Woof, woof!
Biscuit ran and ran.
Oink! Oink!
The piglet ran, too.
Honk! Honk! Honk! Honk!
Now the geese joined the chase. Of course Biscuit liked nothing better than playing chase! He ran past the horse stables and past the cows. He ran past the sheep and past the goats, too. Biscuit led the parade of animals past the hens and past the chickens. He had never had so much fun on the farm before.

Woof!

Biscuit scrambled into the pigpen with the tiny piglet following close behind.

"Silly puppy!" said the little girl. "The piglet is back in the pen at last. And so are you, Biscuit!"

Woof, woof!

Oink!

Biscuit sat with the tiny piglet by his side. It was always fun to help on the farm, but even more fun to make a new friend.

Biscuit Plays Ball

It was beautiful spring morning. The little girl and her friends had made plans to meet at the park to play ball. The little girl put on her baseball cap and sneakers. She carried her favorite bright-blue ball. Then she called to her favorite puppy, "Come along, Biscuit. It's time to go to the park. It's time to play ball."

Woof, woof!

When they arrived at the park, some of their friends were already seated on the bleachers. Others were busy warming up in the field.

"Look, Biscuit," said the little girl. "The game is about to begin."

Woof, woof!

Biscuit bounced the bright-blue ball on his nose. Playing ball was fun!

The little girl knelt down next to Biscuit and stroked his soft fur.

"Sorry, Biscuit," she said. "It's time for me to take the ball now. Sit here. You can watch us play."

Biscuit was always a very obedient puppy.
But right now, he didn't want to sit and watch.
He hurried right over to where the game was
about to begin. He really loved to play ball.

Woof, woof!

"Wait, Biscuit," said the little girl. "Where are you going? You can't play ball now, silly puppy," she said. "There are no dogs in this ball game."

The little girl gently led Biscuit back to a grassy patch where he could sit and watch the game.

"Stay here now, Biscuit," she said. "It's time for us to play ball."

Woof, woof!

Biscuit didn't stay put for long this time, either. When he saw the bright-blue ball go up in the air, he knew he had to play, too!
Woof!

Biscuit hurried over to the little girl and her friends. If only he could reach that ball.
Woof, woof!

"Uh-oh, Biscuit," said the little girl. "Not again!"

Once more, the little girl patiently led Biscuit over to a grassy patch at the park.

"Come along, Biscuit. I know you love to play ball, but I'm afraid there are no dogs in this ball game," she said. "Won't you stay here?" she asked her small puppy. "Please?"

Woof, woof!
Biscuit settled down
in the green grass. This
wasn't going to be easy.

But when a big kick sent the ball flying high through
the air, Biscuit jumped up. Chasing a ball was much more
fun than sitting in the grass! There was only one thing to
do. Biscuit ran as fast as he could . . .

and caught the ball!
Woof, woof! Woof, woof!

The little girl and her friends ran as fast as they could after Biscuit!

"Stop, Biscuit. Come back," the little girl called.

But Biscuit, even more excited than before, just kept running. He ran all around the field, passing first base, second base, third base, and even home plate! The ballplayers could hardly keep up with the fast little puppy!

Woof, woof!

"Oh no, Biscuit," called the little girl. "Come back with the ball!"

Biscuit chased after the ball. He jumped. He pounced. Biscuit rolled with the ball. He held onto the ball in his mouth as he ran and ran.

Woof, woof!

But just when the little girl finally caught up with her mischievous and playful puppy, she noticed that the blue ball was no longer big and round. Instead, the bright-blue ball had a very large hole!

"Silly puppy!" said the little girl.
"There is no air left in the ball.
How can we play now?"

Biscuit looked down at the ball.
Then he looked at the little girl
and wagged his tail.

"It's okay, Biscuit,"
said the little girl.
"We know you
were just playing."
Woof!

Now Biscuit's ears perked up. He heard a sound. It was a very familiar sound.

"Oh, Biscuit," called the little girl, "where are you going now?"

Woof, woof!

Biscuit ran until he found his very best friend, Puddles. Puddles carried a small ball that was just the right size for a ball game. The little girl's friend carried a baseball glove and a baseball bat, too. That gave the little girl an idea!

"Wait a minute," said the little girl. "Maybe
Biscuit was right, after all. Maybe we can all play
ball together," she said.

That sounded like a perfect idea to everyone!

"Are you ready to play
the first puppy ball game ever?"

"Batter up!" came the call from the crowd.

The little girl stood ready with the bat at home plate.
The first pitch was thrown. . . .

Woof, woof!

Who was there to catch it? Biscuit, of course!

"That's the way, Biscuit," the little girl said, giggling.
"You caught the ball!"

Woof!

"I guess we *can* all play ball together, Biscuit," she
said. "Now follow me! We can't forget to run around
the bases, too."

Woof, woof!

Biscuit Loves the Library

"Biscuit, where are you?" called the little girl.

Woof!

Biscuit was soon at her side, happily wagging his tail. Taking a walk was always one of Biscuit's favorite things to do. But today was no ordinary walk. Today the little girl was bringing Biscuit to the library for a very special event.

Together, the little girl and Biscuit walked past the park and the post office. When they turned to enter the doors of the library, Biscuit looked up at the little girl. He was certain he had never been here before. Still, it was always fun to discover someplace new.

"It's a very special day at the library, Biscuit,"
explained the little girl. "Today is Read to a Pet Day!
Everyone can bring along their favorite stuffed animal or
pet to share a story. We'll find a wonderful book together,
and then I can read to you, Biscuit."

Woof, woof!

Biscuit always loved to listen to a story. Just inside the library, Biscuit saw lots of friends sprawled out on the big rug. He saw friends sitting at computers. Most of all, he saw a lot of books! Biscuit was just about to go over and greet his friend Puddles when the little girl gently tugged at his leash.

"Come along, Biscuit," she said. "First we must find a book. Then we can go and read with our friends."

Woof, woof!

The little girl brought Biscuit over to a basket
filled with books.

"See, Biscuit?" she said. "There are books about
bunnies and bears. There are books filled with poems
and books filled with prehistoric dinosaurs, too!"

Woof!

Biscuit scratched at the cover of the book. He saw something that looked good enough to eat!

"Funny puppy!" said the little girl, laughing. "That's not a real bone! That's a picture of a great big dinosaur."

Woof, woof!

"This way, Biscuit," said the little girl, leading Biscuit over to the bookshelves. "There are more books over here."

The little girl searched the shelves for the perfect book to share with Biscuit. But when she turned to check on him, he had already set out to explore the library on his own!

Woof, woof!

"Biscuit! Where are you?" called the little girl as quietly as she could. She didn't want to disturb the other children who were busy reading. But it wasn't long before she saw just what caught Biscuit's eye.

"You found the puppets, Biscuit. Puppets are a
great way to tell a story, but for now, won't you help
me find a book to read?"

Woof!

Biscuit followed behind the little girl, but not for long! Curious as ever, he set out on his own again. This time the little girl found Biscuit holding his furry ear to a pair of headphones.

"See, Biscuit?" said the little girl. "There are even stories we can listen to at the library."

Woof, woof!

"The library is filled with so many choices, Biscuit," said the little girl. "I think I've narrowed it down to these two books. Now, which book will it be?"

Woof, woof!
But once again,
Biscuit was off to explore the
library! He ran past the shelves. He
even ran past his friend Puddles.
"Not again, Biscuit! Wait for me!" called
the little girl.
Woof!

At last the little girl caught up with Biscuit. "Biscuit, you are one very smart puppy!" she said. "You found the librarian. The librarian can always help us to find a book that is just right."

Now the librarian knelt down next to Biscuit. She held up a book that might be of interest to a small yellow puppy. There was even a very similar small yellow puppy right on the cover!

Woof, woof!

"I guess that is the book for us," said the little girl. "All we need to do now is find a comfortable spot so we can read with everyone, Biscuit."

Biscuit padded behind the little girl. There were so many children busy reading to their pets. There were children with teddy bears and kittens. There were children with guinea pigs and rabbits. Another puppy had found a place on the cozy rug. But just then, Biscuit saw something else. Something that looked like an especially perfect place to share a story. . . .

Woof, woof!

"Oh no, Biscuit. Where are you going now?" asked the little girl.

With one big leap, Biscuit jumped right onto a big, comfortable chair!

"Silly puppy," said the little girl, giggling. She curled up right next to Biscuit and gave him a big hug. "You found a book that's just right. You found a cozy spot filled with friends, too. Everyone loves the library, Biscuit," said the little girl. "I think it's the very best place to share a story with you!"

Woof, woof!

Biscuit licked the little girl's cheek and snuggled by her side. He wagged his tail as she opened the book to the first page.

"Aren't you glad we came to Read to a Pet Day at the library, Biscuit?" asked the little girl. "Now, let's read!"

Woof, woof!

Biscuit's First Sleepover

Tonight the little girl and her lovable puppy, Biscuit, were going to have their first sleepover at a friend's house.

After giving her mom a big hug and kiss, the little girl and Biscuit greeted Puddles and his owner, who were both waiting at the door. It was time for the sleepover to begin!

"We have our blankets and our dolls, Biscuit," said
the little girl as she unpacked their bag.

Woof, woof!

"Funny puppy!" she said, "You already found your
bone, too."

"Hooray!" the girls cheered together. "Now it's
time for some sleepover fun!"
Woof, woof!

Biscuit and Puddles scampered off to find their
toys. The girls decided to begin the evening with
some games.

"We can play a lot of games if we stay up all
night," said the little girl.

"That wouldn't be much of a sleepover now
would it?" said her friend, laughing.

The two girls sat down at the kitchen table to play
a board game. They fixed themselves a snack, as well.
In no time at all, both puppies scrambled into the
kitchen. They wanted a snack, too!

"There's a special snack just for you two!" said
the little girl. Both puppies enjoyed a crunchy biscuit
while the girls played their game. When they had
finished, it was time for more sleepover plans.

"We can make up some bedtime stories," suggested the little girl. Her friend quickly agreed.

Bow wow!

Puddles curled up to hear the story. It was a story about a little puppy finding a new home.

"Here, Biscuit!' called the little girl. "You can sit on my lap." But Biscuit was more interested in the popcorn bowl than the story!

Woof, woof!

Bow wow!

"Wait, Biscuit," called the little girl. "The story is not over yet! Where are you going?"

The girls quickly followed their puppies into the bedroom. After brushing their teeth and changing into pajamas, it was time to set up their beds for the sleepover. But Biscuit and Puddles had other ideas.

Bow wow!

"No tugging on the pillows, Puddles."

Woof, woof!

"No tugging on the blankets, Biscuit," said the little girl.

Bow wow!

Woof, woof!

With one leap, both puppies jumped on top of the bed!

"Oh no!" the girls cried together. "Silly puppies! No jumping on the bed! Come along now, Biscuit," said the little girl. "It's time to curl up. It's time for bed."

The girls felt cozy and warm under the blankets. So far their sleepover was really going well. It might have been fun to try to stay up even later, but they could feel their eyelids growing heavy. Everyone was just about ready to drift off to sleep when . . .

Woof, woof, woof, woof!
Biscuit jumped up and ran toward the door!
"Biscuit," called the little girl, "where are you going?

Don't you want to sleep at Puddles's house?"

Biscuit looked at the little girl with his soft brown eyes. He tucked his tail between his legs. The little girl knew that meant Biscuit was not happy. It could even mean that Biscuit was afraid. She gathered her puppy in her arms. Sleeping at someone else's house was not quite the same as sleeping at home. Still, she wanted Biscuit to feel as safe and comfortable as possible.

"Here, sweet puppy," she said, bringing Biscuit close to the window. "This is our first sleepover. But we can make a wish on the stars and say good night to the moon, just like at home."

Woof, woof!

Biscuit was beginning to wag his tail already!

"Look, Biscuit," she said. "We can curl up with our blankets and dolls, too, just like at home."

Woof, woof!

Biscuit curled up with his blanket and tucked it around himself, as he did every night at home. But the little girl knew there was one more thing that would make Biscuit feel safe and sound at the sleepover. She reached into her bag and took out one of her favorite things from home. It was a picture of her mom and dad.

"We can even put a picture of Mom and Dad right by our side, Biscuit," she said. That made Biscuit wag his tail a lot. "I can hardly wait to tell them all about our first sleepover fun!"

In no time at all, the four friends were ready for bed. As a small night-light glowed and the moonlight shone through the window, the little girl whispered, "Sleepy puppies, sweet dreams!"

With a sleepy *woof, woof* and a quiet *bow wow*, everyone was soon fast asleep.

Biscuit's First Beach Day

There was nothing as fun as going to the beach on a warm summer's day. It was Biscuit's first trip to the beach, and it would be fun to watch her puppy dig in the sand and splash in the waves.

"Here we are, Biscuit," said the little girl. "It's a beautiful sunny day. It's a wonderful day to spend at the beach."

Woof, woof!

Standing on the soft sand, the little girl watched as Biscuit sniffed at the salty sea air and wagged his tail at the seagulls flying overhead.

"This way, Biscuit," said the little girl. "We have
our beach blanket and towels. We have a big umbrella
to give us plenty of shade, too."

Woof, woof!

Biscuit was having fun at the beach already.

He tugged gently at the corner of the beach blanket
and helped the little girl set it down in the sand.
"That's the way to help, Biscuit," she said, smiling.
Biscuit sniffed at the sand beneath his paws. He
had never felt anything quite like this before.

"Here, Biscuit," called the little girl. "We can build a sand castle on the beach. I have my pail and shovel."

Woof, woof!

"Funny puppy!" she said. "And you know just how to dig!"

In no time at all, Biscuit was busy digging in the soft, soft sand!

"Be careful, Biscuit," said the little girl. "We don't want to spray anyone with sand."

Woof!

After much digging, stacking, and sculpting, the sand castle was finished at last. Next the little girl took Biscuit for a walk along the seashore. There were lots of interesting things to discover.

"The beach is filled with seashells,
Biscuit," said the little girl. "Let's see how many we can find."
Woof, woof!
Biscuit helped the little girl find shell after shell. Some were striped; some were spotted. Some had unusual and beautiful shapes. But it wasn't long until Biscuit found something else he had never seen before. He bent down low and wagged his tail.

Woof, woof!

"Oh, Biscuit," said the little girl. "You found a starfish."

Woof!

Biscuit was very busy exploring the starfish when the little girl called to him.

"Look, Biscuit! Puddles is here!"

Woof, woof!

Bow wow!

Biscuit ran to his best friend. The beach day was
becoming more fun with every minute.

"This way, everybody," said the little girl. "We can
all go for a dip in the ocean. Are you ready, Biscuit?
Let's jump over the ocean waves together!"

Biscuit stood at the water's edge with the little girl. He watched as the cool ocean water came up and tickled his paws. He watched as the water drifted away again.

"Here comes a wave, Biscuit," said the little girl. "Get ready to jump!"

SPLASH! Into the ocean he went!

Woof, woof! Woof, woof!

Swimming at the beach was even more fun
than swimming at the pond! But when it was
time to come out . . .

Woof!

"Oh no, Biscuit," said the little girl. "Not a
big shake!"

After a refreshing
swim, it was time to dry off
and have lunch. Biscuit and Puddles hurried over to the big
umbrella. Each puppy took a corner of the towel and tugged!

"Silly puppies!" The girls laughed. "No tugging on the
towel. It's time to have a picnic lunch at the beach.
We packed sandwiches, fruit, and
drinks . . . and some special
treats for you, too."

The two girls also set
out a fresh bowl of water
for the puppies to share.
But just as they were
finishing lunch, a
gust of wind blew
their beach ball right
off the towel.

"Oh no!" said the little girl. "There goes our beach ball!"

Woof!

Biscuit set off at once to fetch the ball. He hadn't gone very far when he came face to face with a new friend.

"Good puppy," said the little girl. "You found our beach ball, and you found a seagull, too."

Woof, woof!

The sky was bright and a warm breeze was blowing.

"Follow me," called the little girl.

Woof, woof!

Bow wow!

Biscuit and Puddles watched as the girls let their kite soar up, up, up into the sky.

What could be next for the puppies on such a wonderful beach day?

After a lot of sun and a lot of fun, Biscuit
and Puddles found a shady spot beneath
the large umbrella. They curled
up and took a nap as they listened to
the gentle crash of the waves.

"Sweet puppies," said the little
girl. "The beach is a perfect place
for sun and fun . . . and a little
nap, too!"